This Walker book belongs to:

For Cheri ~W. B. To Ammon and Chloe ~K. H.

First published 2018 by Walker Books Ltd, 87 Vauxhall Walk, London SE11 5HJ • This edition published 2019 • This book has been typeset in ITC Esprit
Printed in China • British Library Cataloguing in Publication Data: a catalogue record for this book is available from the British Library
ISBN 978-1-4063-8312-6 • www.walker.co.uk • 10 9 8 7 6 5 4 3 2 1

THERE'S A DINOSAUR ON THE 13TH FLOOR

Wade Bradford illustrated by Kevin Hawkes

WALKER BOOKS
AND SUBSIDIARIES
LONDON • BOSTON • SYDNEY • AUCKLAND

"Welcome to the Sharemore Hotel," said the porter.
"You must be Mr Snore. Let me show you to your room."

"The sooner the better," said Mr Snore.
"I am very" – YAWN – "sleepy."

"Here you are," said the porter. "Room 104.
Sweet dreams, Mr Snore."

Mr Snore thanked the porter, got ready for bed,
crawled under the covers and switched off the light.

But as he was about to lay his head upon the pillow,
he heard a squeaking sound.

"Hello, front desk? This is Mr Snore in room 104. Somebody is sleeping on my pillow."

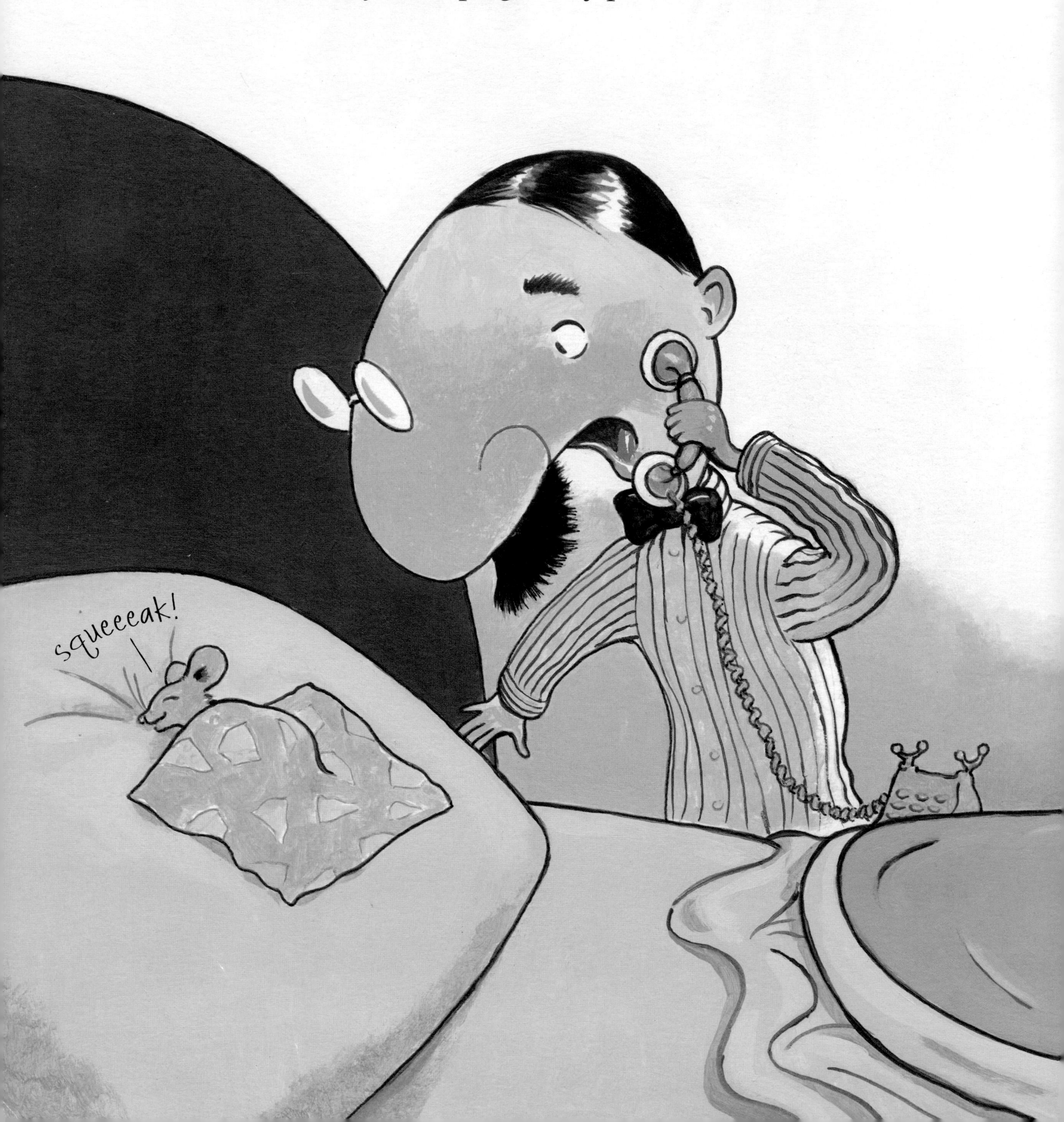

“Yes, that would be the mouse,” said the porter.
“I believe he has had a very long day.”

“So have I,” grumbled Mr Snore. “And I do not wish to share a room with a mouse!”

So the porter led Mr Snore to a room on the second floor.
"Sleep tight, Mr Snore."

Mr Snore crawled into bed and switched off the light, but just as he was falling asleep, he felt a rush of cold air.

Mr Snore called the front desk again. “Someone is hogging all the covers!”

"That would be the pig," said the porter. "Shall I bring you another blanket?"

"No!" Mr Snore fumed. "I want another room!"

So the porter took Mr Snore to the third floor … where there were no pigs or mice to be found.

Mr Snore kicked off his slippers, crawled into bed, and was just about to close his eyes when…

Drip.
Drip.
Drip.

“Sorry about the leaky ceiling,” the porter said as Mr Snore marched past the sea view on the fourth floor.

“This time,” declared Mr Snore, “I will find my own room.”

He found one on the fifth floor.

"I don't think you will like this room," whispered the porter. "Unless, of course, you are fond of—"

“Spiders!” cried Mr Snore.

“Quick,” said the porter. “To the lift!”

"Hamsters! Where are the rest of the giraffes?" asked Mr Snore.

"On the eleventh floor," said the porter.

"Then I will stay on the twelfth," said Mr Snore.

So they went to the twelfth floor. “Hey, it’s empty,” said Mr Snore.

“No one ever stays here,” explained the porter.

“Perfect,” said Mr Snore, and he lay down and shut his eyes.

“It does tend to get a bit noisy,” the porter warned, but Mr Snore was already fast asleep.

STOMP,
STOMP,
STOMP!
Gurgle,
Gurgle.
SWISH,
SWISH.

Mr Snore rang the front desk.

"I cannot sleep with all this noise! I'm going to find a room on the thirteenth floor."

"Oh, dear, no!" said the porter. "On the thirteenth floor there is a—"

Click!

Mr Snore did not wait to hear the porter's warning.
He went up to the thirteenth floor.

There were no mice, no pigs, no penguins, no snakes,
no spiders, no dolphins, no bees and no giraffes.
Not even a hint of a hamster.

Nothing but a giant room with a giant bed and a giant pillow.

"I do hope Mr Snore will be all right," said the porter.

Ring! went the phone at the front desk of the Sharemore Hotel.

"Hello. This is the dinosaur on the thirteenth floor. Somebody is sleeping on my pillow!"

The porter sighed. "That would be Mr Snore," he said. "He has had a very long day."

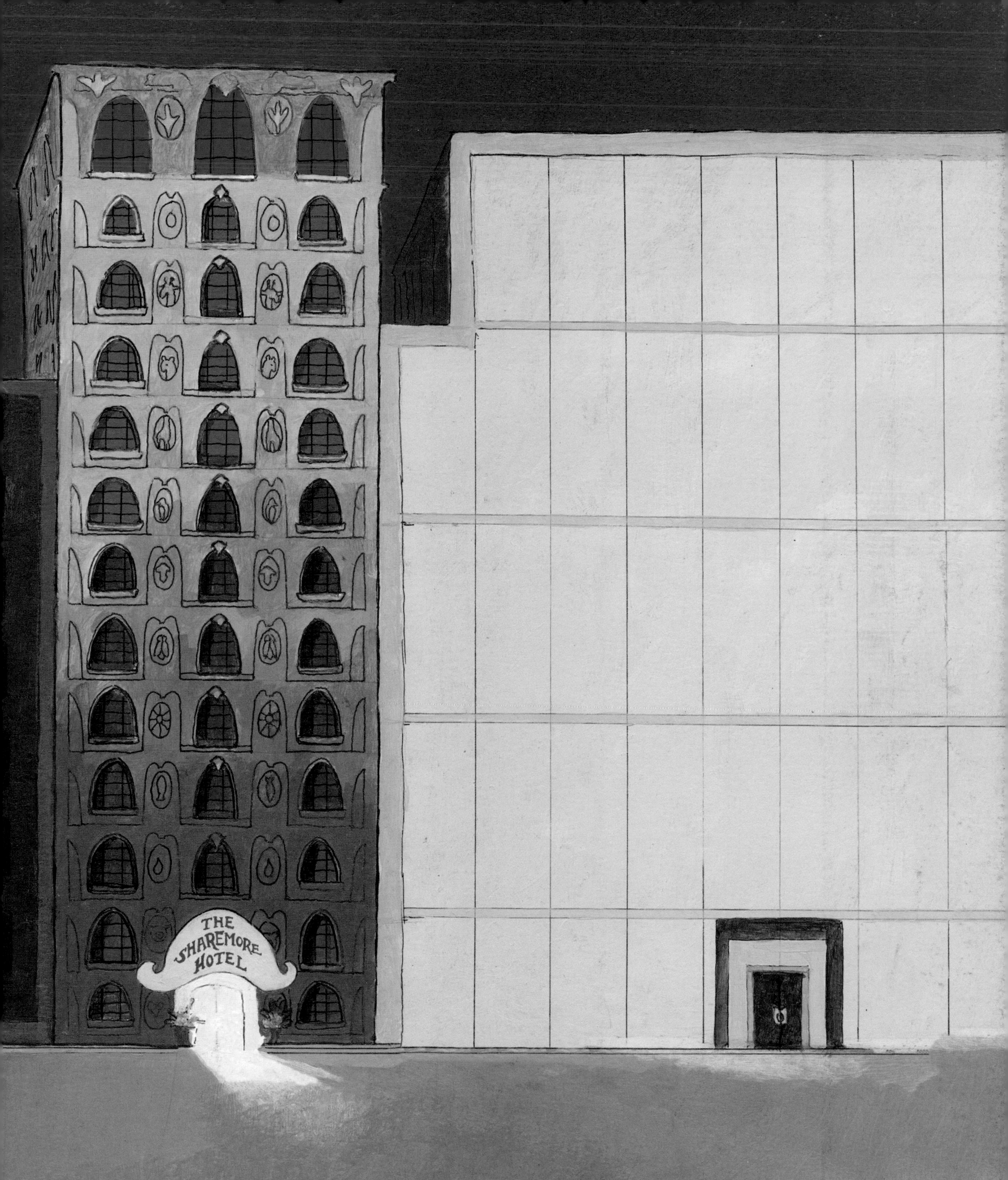
THE
SHAREMORE
HOTEL

Look out for:

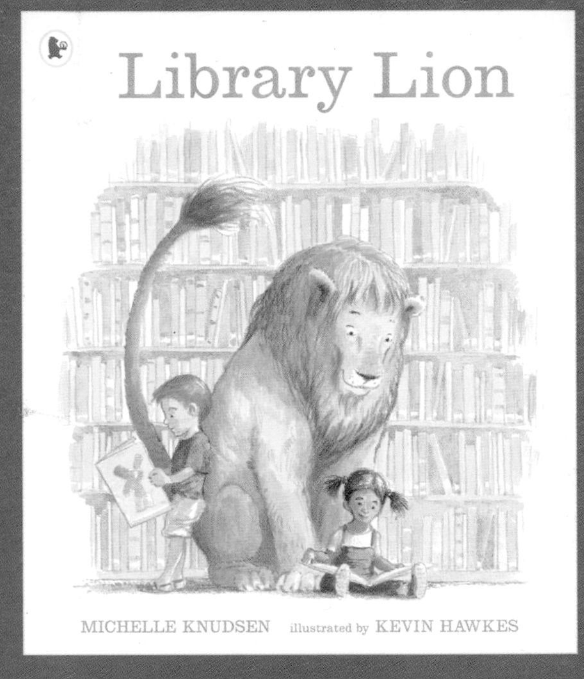

978-1-4063-0567-8

Over 1 million copies sold

A *New York Times* bestseller

A TIME magazine "100 Best Children's Books of All Time" selection

"A warm-hearted story in which Kevin Hawkes's stylishly old-fashioned illustrations capture precisely the feel of how libraries once were" *Guardian*